Nick Sams   Shawna McColligan

Tyler Lamb
Josh Cox

Michael Robinson
Kailynn B

The Cat Has Class!

by

2nd & 4th Grade Franklin Elementary
Center Students, Parkersburg, WV
with
Martin & Delia Wach

The Cat Has Class!

by

2nd & 4th Grade Franklin Elementary Center Students, Parkersburg, WV

with
Martin & Delia Bowman Wach

Dedication

Miss Ellis, Mrs. Davis, and Mrs. Bargeloh would like to thank the students for all of their hard work on this book. We also appreciate the support of both our school and county office staff in this effort. Also a special thank you goes out to Lynne T., Gilda H., Hollie B., Judy M., and Debby L. for going above and beyond the call of duty to complete this project.

---

copyright ©2008 Headline Books

To order additional copies of this book,
for book publishing information,
or to contact the authors:

Headline Books
P.O. Box 52
Terra Alta, WV 26764
www.headlinebooks.com
www.headlinekids.com

Tel/Fax: 800-570-5951
Email: mybook@headlinebooks.com

Headline Kids is an imprint of Headline Books

ISBN 0-929915-71-2
ISBN-13: 978-0-929915-71-5

Library of Congress Control Number: 2007931931

PRINTED IN THE UNITED STATES OF AMERICA

School Programs

To arrange for the Wachs to come to your school call 800-570-5951.

Programs for: K-12, Parents, Parent/ Children, Teachers, Artist In Residence Writing Workshops Collaboration Books [like this one!]

For more information visit www.headlinekids.com

Front Cover Art by Delia Bowman Wach

Triarco™ Art Materials used by the students and Delia Wach for the artwork in this book include:

5 ply white Bristol Board, Artist Tracing Pad, Faber-Casteel™ Watercolor Pencil, Design Ebony pencil set, #2 pencil, White Pearl Eraser, Copy Paper, Triarco™ Artiselect Faux squirrel watercolor brush, Scotch Brand™ removable magic tape, and Sharpie™ Extra Ultra-fine Point Markers.

It doesn't matter what they call me as long as I am fed.
They call me kitty because I am a kitty.

Frankie

They call me friend.

Cat Kitty

My friend hid me in a box of puppets.

Introduction

During a School Show visit to Franklin Elementary Center in Parkersburg, WV we gave them a workshop based on our newest title, *An Adventure in Writing,* about the process of writing a children's book. We also included stories about our adventures in the South American Rain Forest and the creatures that tried to sting, bite and sometimes kill us. We were able to spend the afternoon with students who wanted to become authors and illustrators. We reviewed our process for writing and spent a lot of time brainstorming story ideas trying to come up with a good subject for a book. We explained that good books require a good story and the best stories come from a person's own experience.

There were the usual suggestions of knights, dragons, and magical events.

We asked if anyone had ever met a knight, battled a dragon, or gone to school in a castle in a far away county? We explained that, to write such books of fiction, you have to be very knowledgeable and spend quite a bit of time doing research on your subject. We continued to work to come up with a good story line, but without much success.

At lunch, we had noticed a small cat wandering the school grounds. We had seen a small cat house outside the library entrance and began to ask about this animal. It appeared to be a very well kept secret among everyone at the school and—the cat had become an *unofficial* staff member! The cat had a fantastic home and was cared for by all the kids and some very special teachers. We mentioned the school cat; the lights went on, and the stories began.

So, three very special educators have guided some even more special 2nd and 4th graders to the completion of this children's book. It is a wonderful adventure story and has definitely been "An Adventure in Writing."

Marty and Delia Wach

"Coco Tiger"

They call me "Queen" because I am the queen of food and I am nothing but royalty!

My name is.....well, I have so many names it's wonderful! Can you guess why I have so many names? Here are a few of my names...They call me "Kitty" because I am a kitty. They call me "Queen" because I am the queen of food and I am nothing but royalty!

They call me "Frankie" now instead of "Franklin" because they found out I am a girl.

They call me "Cat LaTeetha" because my meows sound like a beautiful concert.

JC

When they call me "Tub- Tub" are they calling me fat or are they saying I need a bath?

LC

The kids call me "Coco" because I like a cup of coco before I go to sleep with my bedtime story. It doesn't really matter what they call me, as long as I get food. A cup of coco relaxes me. But, if you want me to sleep through the night I need a bedtime story.

I lived in a nice house with a nice family. I had a queen-size pillow. The family was good to me. I was lying on my queen size pillow when big hairy men started carrying boxes out of the house. I hissed, but they didn't stop taking the boxes.

I slipped out to see where the boxes were going. The men were putting the boxes into an enormous truck.

I tried to get into the truck, but the big hairy men stopped me. The big hairy men got into the truck and drove away.

I went back to the house. I couldn't get in. I tried scratching at the door. I tried the back door and side door. I decided to check the windows. I used the kids' mini trampoline to jump and see in the window. On my first landing my claws stuck to the trampoline. I decided that was not my best idea. I got off the trampoline. I went to the old oak tree and climbed up. Once I could see in the window, I realized there was nothing left in the house.

NS

I sat on the porch to wait for my family to return. After a while, I realized they weren't coming back. I started to get hungry and went searching for food.

I saw a mouse and started chasing it. It led me to the woods by a huge mansion full of kids.

The kids must rule the adults because there were more kids than adults. I thought the owner of that place must be rich and have a huge refrigerator. I watched some young ladies go into a building and come out with food.

RH
DS
LC

TB
KB

I wish I had some of that food. WOW! A whole box of tacos, my favorite food!

One of the ladies left the door open. I slipped in and hid in the kitchen for the rest of the day. I fell asleep, but when I woke up there were people with mops cleaning the floor. I got scared and ran out of that room.

I started to wander around the mansion. A lady saw me. I tried to hide, but she said, "Come on Kitty, don't be afraid."
I wasn't sure. She got a bowl and put in some tacos.
She walked around the corner, but left the bowl of tacos.
Should I or shouldn't I?

I should! I walked very slowly to the bowl as the smell was drawing me closer. I was shivering with fear and hunger as I looked to make sure the coast was clear.

As soon as I saw the coast was clear, I darted for the bowl. I ate the tocos and that is why they call me "Pedro" because I love tacos and morocco's.

After eating I felt better. I thought I could trust her now so I went off to find her and to thank her.

I found her cleaning the mansion's bathroom. I rubbed up against her leg to say thank you. Then, I allowed her to pet me.

I followed her around the mansion as she was cleaning. She went back and got me some milk.

I heard another person. I was terrified and hid behind my new friend. I heard a voice say, "Judy."

My new friend hid me in a box of puppets.

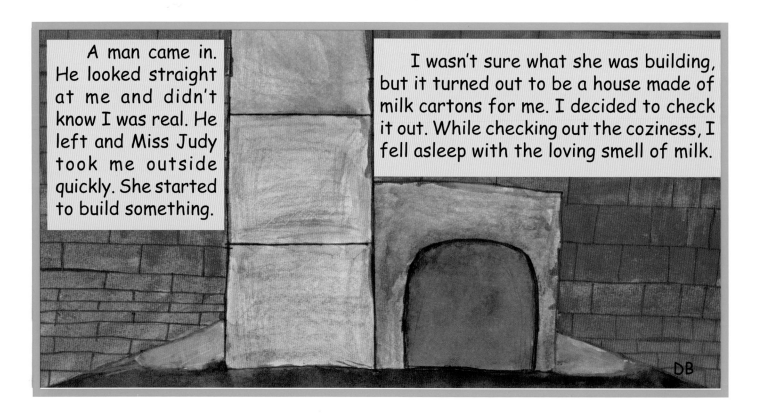

A man came in. He looked straight at me and didn't know I was real. He left and Miss Judy took me outside quickly. She started to build something.

I wasn't sure what she was building, but it turned out to be a house made of milk cartons for me. I decided to check it out. While checking out the coziness, I fell asleep with the loving smell of milk.

I woke up with a cool breeze in my face and wiggled myself to keep warm and fell back asleep.

Well, I'm finally settled in here at the mansion. I really like it here. Then I started seeing my picture on the walls.

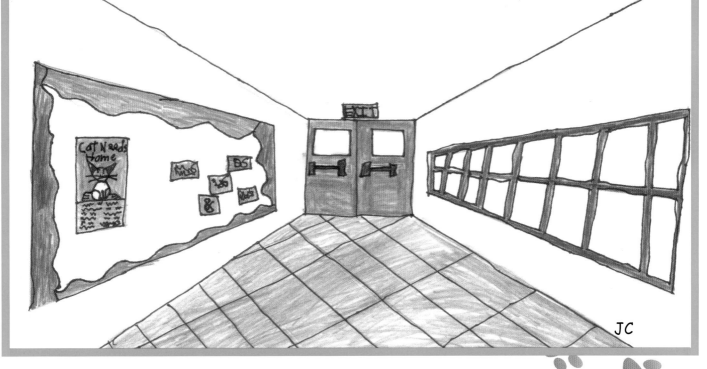

One day a little girl got out of a blue car. She picked me up and put me in the car. When we got to her house, I tried to escape. But it didn't work. I waited and planned my escape for nightfall so they wouldn't see me in the dark. I planned to use my concert meows like I needed to go out. Then, I would make my escape.

AR
KB

They let me out. I noticed they had a wooden fence. I thought no problem. So, I just climbed to the top of the fence. Whoa! There's a big dog on the other side. I needed to think of something. I used my concert meows to distract the dog until I got to the other side of the fence.

Once I cleared the yard, I ran for the road. I started my trip back to the mansion. I got on the road and backtracked where the car had gone. As I slowly remembered what I saw from the car, I started running toward the mansion.

When I got back to the mansion I took a long nap because my legs were tired.

A delightful smell of breakfast pizza woke me later that morning. I jumped up on the windowsill and used my concert voice. If my food memory serves me right, these are the same young ladies who had my favorite food TACOS! I heard footsteps behind me, and suddenly there was food for me.

I waited all day for the kids to come out of the mansion. A boy came by, picked me up, put me in a car and off I went AGAIN!

This ride was longer than the last ride. It's going to take me longer to get back to the mansion.

DSc

I said to myself "Plan 2." After the family left in the morning I started snooping around without a care. I wanted to let the family that took me from my mansion know that I am nothing but royalty.

I jumped onto the mantel above the fireplace and knocked off the pictures and other valuables. There, that should do it!

LC

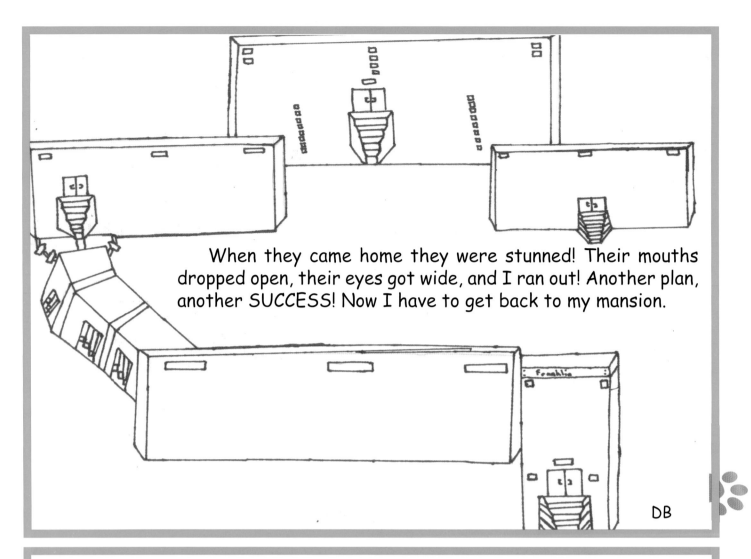

When they came home they were stunned! Their mouths dropped open, their eyes got wide, and I ran out! Another plan, another SUCCESS! Now I have to get back to my mansion.

DB

I started walking knowing it was going to be a long journey back. I saw a big building. Suddenly I recognized my mansion. I started running to it. I saw some kids on the playground.

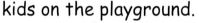

I raced to see Miss Judy. I began to smell around for my house of milk cartons. I walked all the way around the mansion, but couldn't find my house.

I began to think, "What if they forgot about me? Didn't they think I would come back? Surely they knew I would return."

I started looking around for my pictures on the walls. Just in case they took them down, I started to look for the big sign with the falcon on it

I walked toward the kids. These weren't the kids at my mansion. So I turned, leaving to look for my house, the one Miss Judy made for me out of milk cartons. I really could use some milk right now.

There is only one room I couldn't forget, the lunch room. I went looking for that room to get some food and find my milk carton house.

After I realized this wasn't my mansion I walked away toward the road. I was scared and started looking both ways. I looked for cars. One popped out of nowhere. It almost hit me! I got out of the way just in time.

JG

NS

After walking for a while, I began to wonder if I was ever going to get back to my mansion. I darted to the other side of the road and went to the sidewalk. I started walking again.

I had to hunt for my food. During a break by a creek, I discovered fish.

NS

I decided to stay and feast on fish. That restored my energy and I stayed a few days. But, I still wanted to get back to my mansion and my "Miss Judy."

After a few days, I was taking another break near some woods. There was a house nearby. I didn't get too close to the house, but a lady saw me and put out some food.

I thought of Miss Judy and the bowl of tacos. I don't want to be put in a house again, so I waited to see if she would stay or go back in the house.

She went back in the house and I thought, *Cool, she didn't try to catch me.*

JG

DS

I climbed up into a tree. I looked around and saw another mansion. This might not be my mansion either. I decided to check it out. I climbed down the tree and walked to this mansion. I looked for the sign with the falcon on it. But, I didn't see it. I walked around to the other side of the mansion. Then I saw it! The sign with the falcon was there.

I said, "Hooray! I'm back!"

I went to the door using my concert voice. For a minute I thought Miss Judy wasn't coming.

I waited and then she came to the door. She said, "You're back, Kitty." She picked me up and took me inside for a bowl of milk and my favorite food, TACOS!

KM

TC

After eating, she took me to the library while she cleaned. I found my puppet friends in the box as usual. I decided to hop in and join them for a nice long nap.

I woke up in my house of milk cartons. Miss Judy must have put me here. She even thought to tuck in the moroccos which were a gift from the puppets.

I celebrated my return by shaking my maroccos and eating tacos. I was standing there eating the tacos and shaking the moroccos when Mrs. Bargeloh came by and called me "Pedro." She asked, "How did you get the puppets' moroccos?" I tried to tell her that the puppets gave them to me as a welcome home gift.

I started walking around the mansion. I looked in the first building and sat on the window sill. I heard the adult, Miss Ellis, say, "Reading everyone."

All the children got out the books and started saying the same words. I guess that must be reading. I listened to a story about a man who traveled around the world. The adult held up a picture of the man looking at signs. The signs looked like what I saw when I was trying to get back to my mansion.

I figured out that if I learned to read, it wouldn't take me as long to get back to my mansion from another car trip if I had to.

I decided right then and there that I was going to stay and learn how to read.

Everyday I went to that room to learn to read. When the kids left my mansion at the end of the day, I would go to my house for a nice long nap.

One day I heard a BANG! I woke up in an instant to see what the noise was. I saw Miss Judy standing by a big green box. She had black bags in her hands. She put them in the big green box, closed the lid and it shut with another BANG!

TL

Then Miss Judy took me inside and fed me salmon. When she put me outside, she put a bowl of fresh water outside with me. That night I woke up because I was freezing. I went to take a drink of water. I suddenly realized my water was an icicle.

I have to devise Plan 3. This plan has to give me a way to get inside and stay! The next night after Miss Judy fed me I acted like I was sick. She carried me with her to every room she cleaned. I'm finally getting a tour of my mansion in royal style.

I could get used to this place. I think I could live like this.

When Miss Judy got ready to go home, I ran to the Reading Room. It is cozy and I can read most of the signs and books in this room. I heard Miss Judy upstairs looking for me in the room with the box of puppets. Another plan tried and SUCCEEDED!

I know I am not supposed to be here, but I know there is more to learn than what I already know. For instance, I really don't know what the signs on the road mean. I also don't want to forget about the stocked refrigerator. What I enjoy most is having a cool, cute second grader read to me. This room is the perfect place for me to stay.

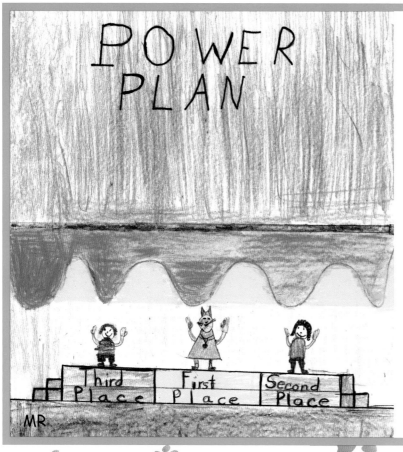

It's time for Plan 4. The best plan of all! I like to call this plan, 'My Power Plan,' because this time if it would work, I can stay here forever. I found a comfy pillow and slept a little bit. I could barely sleep through the night since I didn't have my coco and my bedtime story.

I woke to the fresh smell of breakfast pizza. As soon as an adult arrived, I ran out the door. I went to get my breakfast. Since I have been back I don't usually have to sing for my meals.

While I was waiting for reading class I saw another cat. We became friends and I decided to play with my new friend. This time when I talked to this friend she said something back. She's not like my puppet friends; I think they are shy.

I thought it might be close to reading time so I went to the windowsill and stayed there for Reading Class. I was learning some really neat stuff. But I still wanted in my mansion.

Since today was nice outside, the window was open. I knew I had to take this chance. I crept into the classroom and hid on a chair under a big desk. I knew I would be safe here.

Then an adult said it was time for silent reading. I hadn't heard of that before. So, I listened. I didn't hear a sound. The adult came toward the big desk. I thought, "Oh, no, if she sits down I'll be discovered." I jumped off the chair and ran swiftly and quietly to the nearest corner.

There was a plant I hid behind. The door opened and I smelled food. I peeked out from behind the plant and saw the adult writing. She didn't see me.

I went to the door and tried to get out. But the door was closed. I am going to have to use my concert voice to get her attention. She finally looked at me and without thinking she put me out the door into the hallway. I followed the scent of the food and heard the noises. I went to the room and there were kids starting to eat. Another adult came in and a kid said, "Hi, Mrs. Davis."

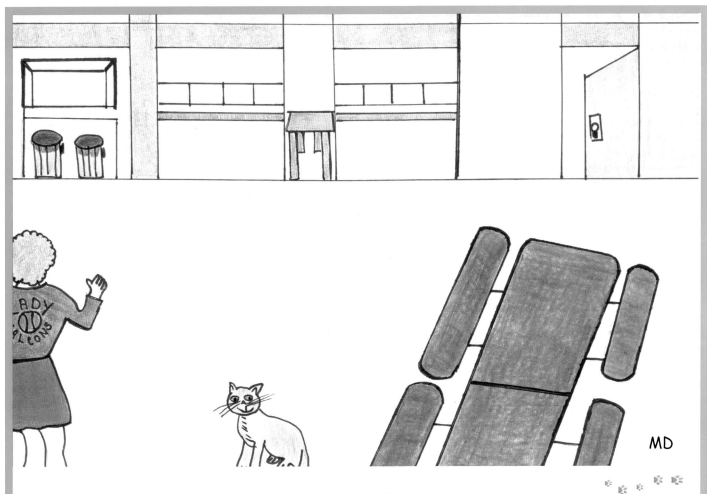

She let out a scream. Then she said, "A cat! What is a cat doing in the cafeteria?" She carefully picked me up and said, "It is time for the children's lunch and you can have your lunchtime later." She put me outside and later she came out and fed me. After my lunch I went back to my house and took my nap.

MH

"Seafood Sally"

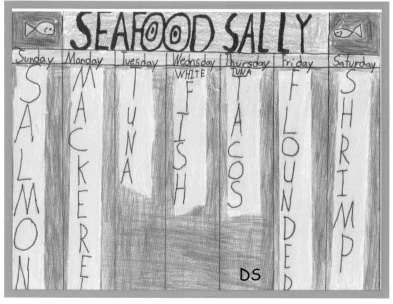

Miss Judy fed me and I had mackerel. So today must be Mackerel Monday. Seafood Sally is a good name because each day of the week I have a different dinner.

That evening I was taking my stroll in the woods when I smelled smoke from my mansion. I quickly ran toward my mansion. I hid under the big green box. I couldn't believe my eyes. My cozy house was on fire! Where am I going to sleep tonight? I decided to stay under the big green box tonight. Maybe Miss Judy can help me tomorrow.

When Miss Judy came to work she started looking for me right away. She told me, "Don't worry Frankie, we'll get you a new home." She was right! I got a new home that is more comfy *and* warmer. I even got a new pillow that is softer, cozier and larger. If they built me a new home I guess I am going to stay awhile. But I really want to be inside my mansion.

So I now need Plan 5, maybe it would be best to do it tomorrow after I rest. I'm tired now and my pillow is so cozy.

If you want to hear another story, come back and visit me. I'll be here learning new things and caring for my new family...

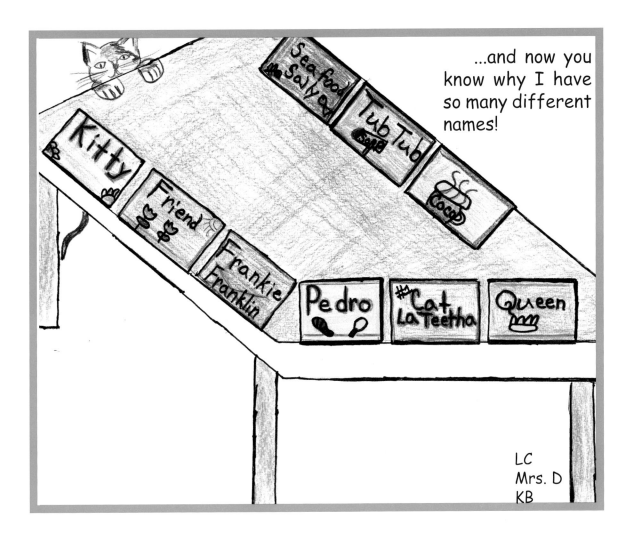

...and now you know why I have so many different names!

The History of the Cat
Mrs. K. F-Bargeloh L/M Specialist

The cat has been around Franklin Elementary Center off and on for about six years. She is about nine years old and missing a lot of teeth. This story is based on true events that have occurred over the years at our school. She does answer to all the different names in this book, according to who calls her.

I would also like to add my congratulations to the students for doing this project. They said, "Why can't we?" and they proved it could be done!

Appreciation Note
Miss Ellis 2nd Grade and Mrs. Davis 4th Grade

We would like to take this time to express our gratitude to the students for all of their hard work and dedication to this project. Also a thank you to the school staff for all of their support.

These students worked together and accomplished so much we had faith in their abilities. We hope they had fun and will enjoy sharing their book with others. This project provided so many learning opportunities for all of us.

A very special thanks to "Miss Judy" without whom none of this would be possible. To cat lovers everywhere, we hope you enjoy reading this story!

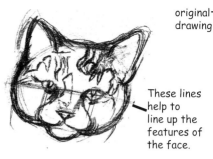

original drawing

1. Do a pencil [32 Office pencil] drawing and work out all the problems. Use while eraser to correct.

These lines help to line up the features of the face.

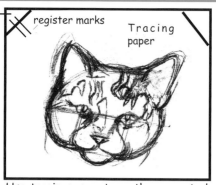

register marks

Tracing paper

2. Use tracing paper, trace the corrected drawing. Mistakes are only problems so keep working them out.

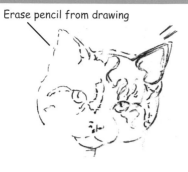

Erase pencil from drawing

3. Take traced image and transfer to Briston Board with graphite paper. Use safe release tape to hold traced image and sandwich with graphic paper.

Use #7 paint brush

4. Begin with your washes—work with washes so the color is transparent. Use the lid of the paint box to thin down the paint with water.

5. When the yellow wash is dry—add a layer of orange.

6. Wash of red.

7. Brown Wash.

8. Add green to the eyes and blue for some shadows.

9. Then, add black. You are finished!

The students at Franklin took on the challenge of using water colors and these are the materials they used for this book:

8 color oval water color set   white eraser   Ultra Fine Sharpie™
#5 faux squirrel brush   Bristol Board   Graphite Paper
#7 camel brush   #2 office pencil
8 1/2" x 11" copy paper   blue safe release tape

The above steps show how the students created the illustrations for their book.

First pencil sketches were made on cheap copy paper. Cheap paper lets you be creative—no pressure to be perfect.

DRAW

cats~~dog

Keep it Simple!

Step 1. Draw with a No. 2 office pencil

Erase pencil lines.

Step 2. Go over pencil with pen.

Step 3. Add one color at a time. Let dry between colors.

Don't let wet paint touch wet paint. Paint one color at a time.

If you are in a hurry, use a hairdryer between colors. It's okay to let colors overlap.

watercolors Bristol board

31

Miss Elizabeth Ellis **2nd Grade Class**	Mrs. Monica Davis **4th Grade Class**
Garrett Adkins	Devin Blair
Kailynn Barker	Kyle Carpenter
Jeremiah Blosser	Tia Carpenter
Tommy Bosely	Lilly Cottle
Tylor Carpenter	Josh Cox
Caleb Deem	Joe Gwynn
Kyle Farrell	Matt Hendrick
Aaron Flanagon	Ronald Hicks
Sierra Leasure	Jake Knotts
Tyler Sanford	Tyler Lamb
Allison Yates	Shawna McColligan
	Kathy Milam
	Andrew Neal
	Andrew Reynolds
	Michael Robinson
	Nick Sams
	David Scruggs
	Dakota Stevens
	Triston Sutten

Special Artists and Helpers

Mrs. Kathryn F. Bargeloh, Library/Media Specialist
Fifth Graders: Dustin Bonnett & Ben Life
Sixth Graders: Hollie Burrows & Judy McColligan
Community Service Workers: Brian Blanc & Danielle Oyler
School Attendence Officer: Miss Lynn T.
TIS person: Mrs. Gilda Haddox
The "Real" Miss Judy—Judy Stienbecker

SM